Grandma Comes to Stay

Written by Jill Eggleton
Illustrated by Kelvin Hawley

"I have come
to stay,"
said Grandma.

"I have bags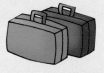

and boxes."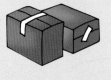

"I have
my plants,"

said Grandma.

"I have my fish.

I have my birds.

And I have
my mice."

The children put

the bags

and boxes

in the house.

"Wow!"

said the children.

"We can not see
the window."

The children put

the plants  in

the house. They put

the fish and

the birds and

the mice

in the house!

"Wow!"
said the children.

"We can not see
the bed!"

Where can
Grandma stay?

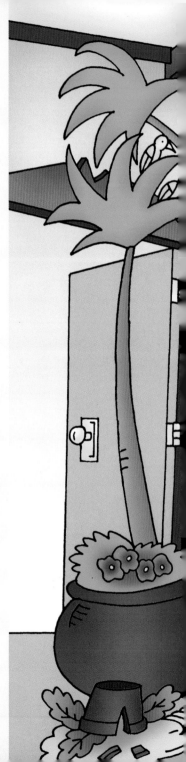

"Here,"
said Grandma.

"Come and
look at me.
This is where
I will stay."

"Wow!"

said the children.
"We will stay here, too!"

Labels

Guide Notes

Title: Grandma Comes to Stay

Stage: Early (2) – Yellow

Genre: Fiction

Approach: Guided Reading

Processes: Thinking Critically, Exploring Language, Processing Information

Written and Visual Focus: Labels

Word Count: 109

THINKING CRITICALLY

(sample questions)

- What do you think this story could be about?
- Focus on the title and discuss.
- Discuss what is unusual in the cover illustration.
- Why do you think Grandma brought so many things when she came to stay?
- What do you think Grandma could have had in all the boxes and bags?
- What else do you think the children could have done with the boxes and bags?
- Why do you think the children wanted to sleep in the tent?

EXPLORING LANGUAGE

Terminology

Title, cover, illustrations, author, illustrator

Vocabulary

Interest words: bags, boxes, plants, birds, mice, tent, wow

High-frequency words (reinforced): come, to, I, have, said, and, my, the, put, in, can, not, they, we, here, look, at, me, this, is, will, too

Positional word: in

Print Conventions

Capital letter for sentence beginnings and names (**G**randma), periods, quotation marks, commas, question marks, exclamation marks